Library of Congress Cataloging-in-Publication Data · Ernst, Lisa Campbell Squirrel Park/Lisa Campbell Ernst. —1st American ed. p. cm. Summary: Stuart clashes with his father, a developer, over the design of a park that threatens an ancient oak tree where his squirrel friend Chuck lives. ISBN 0-02-733562-3 [1. Squirrels-Fiction. 2. Parks-Fiction. 3. Conservation of natural resources-Fiction. 4. Fathers and Sons-Fiction.] I. Title PZ7.E7323Sq 1993 [E] - dc20 92-27920 CIP AC

Maxwell Macmillan Canada, Inc. 1200 Eglinton Avenue East Suite 200. Don Mills, Ontario M3C 3N1 · Macmillan Publishing Company is part of the Maxwell Communications Group of Companies. First edition Printed and bound in Japan 10 9 8 7 6 5 4 3 2 1

The text of this book was set in Goudy Old Style. The illustrations were rendered in pastel, ink, and pencil.

for Sally and Will

SQUIRREL PARK

LISA CAMPBELL ERNST

Bradbury Press   New York

Maxwell Macmillan Canada   Toronto
Maxwell Macmillan International
New York   Oxford   Singapore   Sydney

To most people in Springdale, Chuck and
Stuart were an unlikely pair of best friends.
Sure, they had their differences. But they also had
a lot in common. Like climbing trees, collecting
leaves, and—most importantly—loving the ancient,
gnarled oak tree that grew in the center of town.

For Chuck the magnificent tree was *home*. He grew up in its strong branches, and he played, ate, and slept there.

As the town of Springdale grew, its old trees were chopped down one by one, to make room for new buildings. Finally, Chuck's was the last giant to escape the builder's plans.

Even as the other squirrels left town for more trees, Chuck remained loyal. "This tree is my home," he insisted. "Forever."

Stuart loved the tree as well, from the smell of its fresh new buds in spring, to the veiny old bark that told of the tree's long history.

It was Stuart's father—Mr. Ivey—who had built the new buildings in town, and they were just like him: big, straight, and powerful. Stuart was none of those things.

"Out with the old, in with the new!" Mr. Ivey thundered as the trees were cut down to make room for his buildings. "Someday, Stuart, you will follow in my footsteps!" Mr. Ivey told his son.

Stuart shuddered at the thought. "I promise I'll protect your tree," he told Chuck, "no matter what."

Then one morning Stuart's father broke the calm. "STUART!" he roared from the base of the tree.

"Yes, Dad?" Stuart called timidly.

Mr. Ivey frowned. "Son, you know I don't approve of you lollygagging here with that—that *rodent*," he shouted, "but since you insist, I've decided…we will build a park here."

Mr. Ivey rushed on. "This is your first job, Stuart. *You* will design the park."

"But how?" Stuart asked.

"Draw a picture," Mr. Ivey instructed, "of how the park should look. You will show your drawing at the town meeting this Saturday. Then the park will be built just that way."

Mr. Ivey turned to leave. "This is an important job, son," he called back. "Don't let me down."

At first Chuck and Stuart just stared at each other in disbelief.
"A park!" Stuart shouted at last, and the two friends began to dance
around the tree. Chuck leapt and twirled.

"We'll plant a hundred *more* trees!" cried Stuart. "Walnut! Pecan! Chestnut! And we'll make nature paths, and a playground...."

Chuck looked up into the mass of swaying, dancing leaves above him. And just for a second, he could have sworn he saw the tree smile.

The next morning, Chuck and Stuart got busy—Saturday's town meeting was two days away. Drawing their plot of land, Stuart filled pages with curving, curling paths, with playgrounds and flowers. Chuck dipped his paws in green ink and marked where each tree would be planted. At the center of it all, they drew their spectacular tree.

"Perfect," Stuart said proudly. And Chuck agreed.

Suddenly, though, Mr. Ivey burst into the room. "I see I'm just in time!" he roared, and thrust a strange-looking box into Stuart's hands.

"For your drawing!" Mr. Ivey shouted, taking out two strange wooden tools and sweeping Chuck and Stuart's artwork off the table.

Mr. Ivey demonstrated how to slide a pencil along the edge of one tool to draw a flat, straight line. With the other tool, he drew straight lines at an angle, and straight lines up and down.

"Beautiful!" Mr. Ivey sang. "You will demonstrate these tools at the town meeting. Like father, like son!"

"But—" Stuart began, "I thought curved paths would look nice with the tree." Chuck quickly nodded.

"Nonsense!" Mr. Ivey barked on his way out the door. "With all of my straight buildings in town, I need a park to match."

Stuart stared blankly at Mr. Ivey's drawing and tools. "Now what?" he asked glumly.

Chuck led him back to the tree, in answer.

Unrolling the drawing there, Stuart discovered Mr. Ivey had drawn paths straight through the tree. "We'll have to change that," Stuart gasped, curving the paths around it.

As Chuck chattered his approval, Stuart drew more: playgrounds and curving paths mixed in with Mr. Ivey's straight ones. Soon Chuck got busy with the green ink. And again, at the center of it all, they drew their fabulous tree.

The next morning, Chuck and Stuart bounded into Mr. Ivey's office with their drawing.

"Our park!" Stuart proudly sang. "For tomorrow's town meeting!"

Mr. Ivey frowned at what he saw.

"We used some of the straight lines from your tools," Stuart quickly pointed out, explaining about the path through the tree, "and added our own curved ones—"

"But the tools' lines were *perfect!*" Mr. Ivey interrupted. "Who cares about that old tree?"

Hearing that, Chuck leapt to his feet. CRASH! Three bottles of ink toppled over.

"Out!" Mr. Ivey shouted as the ink swam across their artwork. "Both of you! I'll do a new drawing myself!"

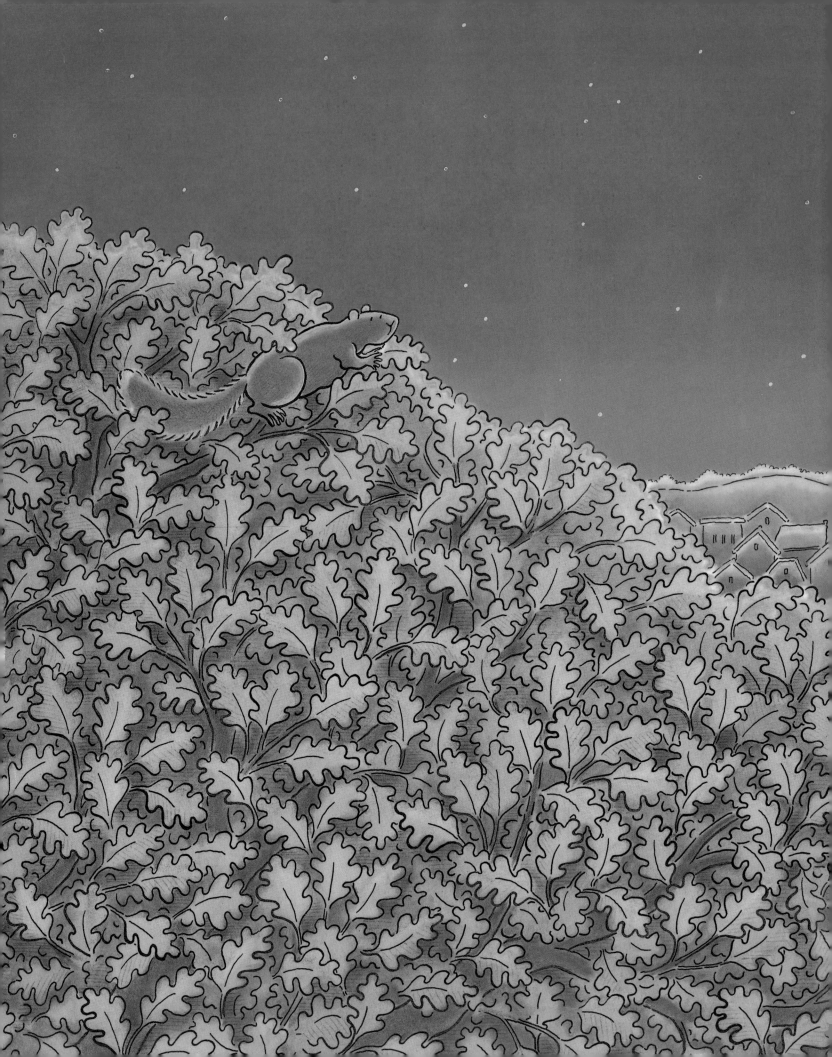

Stuart's father sent him straight home, so Chuck sat alone, at the top of the tree.

"Don't worry" was the last thing Stuart had said.

But Chuck *was* worried. He could still hear Mr. Ivey's voice asking, "Who cares about that old tree?"

"*I* do!" Chuck now called out. "*I* care!" By nightfall, Chuck was frantic.

Suddenly, Chuck saw Mr. Ivey leave his office, carrying the tools and his new drawing. Disappearing into the town hall, he reappeared moments later, empty-handed.

Chuck now sprang into action.

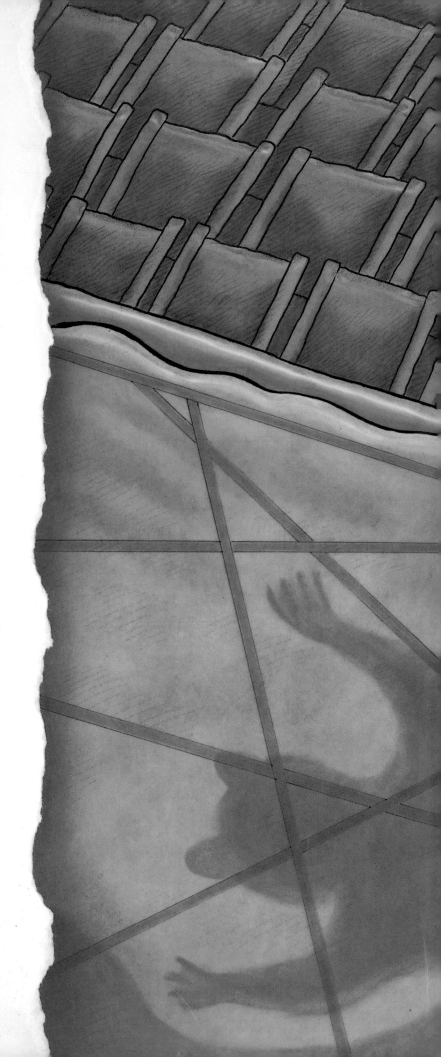

Racing to the town hall, Chuck squeezed through the mail slot. "That drawing is here somewhere," he said.

And he was right. There in the great hall, it sat with Mr. Ivey's tools and art supplies, ready for the demonstration. Chuck inched past the rows of empty chairs until one giant leap landed him square in the middle of the park drawing.

He quickly surveyed the park at his feet—straight paths, a puny playground, no flowers at all. But it was not until Chuck moved off the center of the drawing that he realized the worst: *His tree was not there.*

Chuck could not believe his eyes. He frantically searched the paper—surely the tree was somewhere. But it was not. His tree was to be cut down.

"Don't panic," Chuck told himself. "*Do* something."

First Chuck rolled up Mr. Ivey's drawing and buried it in the pot of a fern nearby. "That takes care of that," he announced.

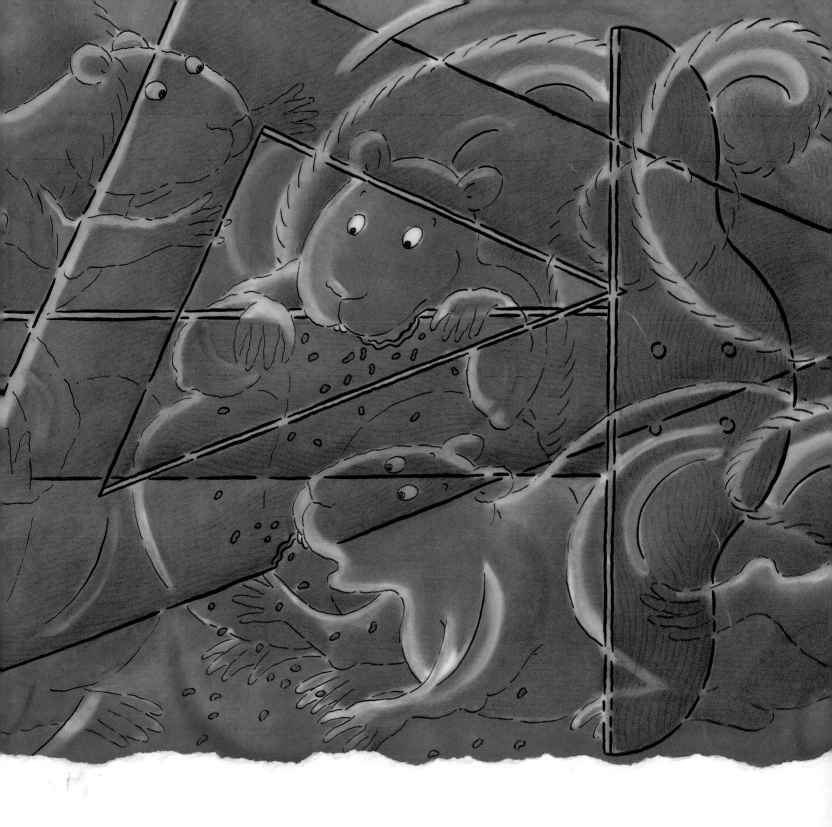

But turning around, Chuck eyed the tools and art supplies. "He'll make another one," Chuck realized, "just like it."

"Unless…" Chuck said, picking up a wooden tool and smelling it. "Maybe…" Suddenly the town hall was filled with a sound that would continue all through the night.

The sound of nibbling.

When Stuart and his father arrived at the town hall the next morning, an excited crowd waited.

Mr. Ivey strode proudly to the front. "Ladies and gentlemen!" he called. "I present…your park!" And with that, he turned to reach for his drawing.

Suddenly, the fast-talking Mr. Ivey was speechless. "The—the *tools*," he stammered at last. "My *drawing*!" A paper with Chuck's tree—drawn on with tiny green pawprints—lay there. Mr. Ivey turned white.

As the hushed crowd waited expectantly, Stuart spied Chuck hiding in the potted fern, and understood. "May I have your attention," Stuart timidly called, rushing forward.

All eyes now turned to Stuart.

"My father," he quietly began, "has made many wonderful buildings in Springdale—and now a park. Today he has asked me to demonstrate his new tools, created specially for this important park design."

The townspeople clapped, and Mr. Ivey, still dumbstruck, stood silently by. Sliding his pencil along one tool, Stuart began to draw curving, curling paths around Chuck's tree.

As the drawing grew, Stuart talked—about flowers, playgrounds, and nature paths, of new trees and the hope for more squirrels. Mostly, though, he talked about the amazing, ancient tree that was older than the town itself.

By the time Stuart was finished, the townspeople—and Chuck— had jumped to their feet, cheering.

But all of this time, Mr. Ivey stood by, silently watching, listening.

"Mr. Ivey!" the mayor finally called. "Speak to us of your very unusual, very beautiful design!"

Slowly Mr. Ivey stepped forward, first looking at the smiling townspeople, then at the drawing. He shook his head, he hunched his shoulders, he waved his arms. At last he turned to Stuart. "What can I say?" he whispered. "Only my very unusual son could make such an unusual drawing. But you are right. It *is* beautiful."

The townspeople—and Chuck—cheered again.

The park was, indeed, built just like Chuck and Stuart's design. In fact, it became so loved, that soon towns all across the country wanted parks the same. Stuart and Mr. Ivey were quick to oblige, using Chuck's very special tools.

With the passing years, Stuart and Chuck could still be found sitting happily in their grand old tree. From its branches they watched as the other trees grew, and squirrels arrived to make their homes. At last the park, with its squirrels, became so treasured that the townspeople affectionately named it Squirrel Park.